WARWICK PUBLIC LIBRARY

W9-BRX-441

DISCARDED AND
WITHDRAWN FROM
WARWICK PUBLIC
LIBRARY

Dear Parent:

Congratulations! Your child is taking the first steps on an exciting journey. The destination? Independent reading!

STEP INTO READING® will help your child get there. The program offers five steps to reading success. Each step includes fun stories and colorful art. There are also Step into Reading Sticker Books, Step into Reading Math Readers, Step into Reading Phonics Readers, Step into Reading Write-In Readers, and Step into Reading Phonics Boxed Sets—a complete literacy program with something to interest every child.

Learning to Read, Step by Step!

Ready to Read Preschool–Kindergarten
• big type and easy words • rhyme and rhythm • picture clues
For children who know the alphabet and are eager to begin reading.

Reading with Help Preschool–Grade 1
• basic vocabulary • short sentences • simple stories
For children who recognize familiar words and sound out new words with help.

Reading on Your Own Grades 1–3
• engaging characters • easy-to-follow plots • popular topics
For children who are ready to read on their own.

Reading Paragraphs Grades 2–3
• challenging vocabulary • short paragraphs • exciting stories
For newly independent readers who read simple sentences with confidence.

Ready for Chapters Grades 2–4
• chapters • longer paragraphs • full-color art
For children who want to take the plunge into chapter books but still like colorful pictures.

STEP INTO READING® is designed to give every child a successful reading experience. The grade levels are only guides. Children can progress through the steps at their own speed, developing confidence in their reading, no matter what their grade.

Remember, a lifetime love of reading starts with a single step!

For Flora Jean
—L.F.

To Gabi, my favorite Lilliputian
—A.J.C.

Text copyright © 2010 by Lisa Findlay
Illustrations copyright © 2010 by Antonio Javier Caparo

All rights reserved.
Published in the United States by Random House Children's Books, a division of Random House, Inc., New York.

Step into Reading, Random House, and the Random House colophon are registered trademarks of Random House, Inc.

Visit us on the Web!
www.stepintoreading.com

Educators and librarians, for a variety of teaching tools, visit us at
www.randomhouse.com/teachers

Library of Congress Cataloging-in-Publication Data
Findlay, Lisa.
Gulliver in Lilliput / adapted by Lisa Findlay ; illustrated by Antonio Javier Caparo.
   p. cm. — (Step into reading. A step 3 book)
Summary: On a voyage in the South Seas, an Englishman finds himself shipwrecked in Lilliput, a land of people only six inches high.
ISBN 978-0-375-86585-5 (trade pbk.) — ISBN 978-0-375-96585-2 (lib. bdg.)
[1. Fantasy. 2. Voyages and travels—Fiction. 3. Size—Fiction.] I. Caparo, Antonio Javier, ill.
II. Swift, Jonathan, 1667–1745. Gulliver's travels. III. Title.
PZ7.F4956665Gu 2010
[E]—dc22 2009027680

Printed in the United States of America

10 9 8 7 6 5 4 3 2 1

Random House Children's Books supports the First Amendment and celebrates the right to read.

STEP INTO READING®

STEP 3

Gulliver in Lilliput

by Lisa Findlay

illustrated by Antonio Javier Caparo

Random House 🏠 New York

Hello. My name is Gulliver.

I am from England.

But I have traveled to many

strange and wonderful lands.

I used to be a doctor
on a sailing ship.
It was a good life,
but it was full of danger.

One terrible day,
there was a great storm at sea.
The wind howled.
The waves crashed.
Our ship was smashed to pieces.

I swam and swam until my arms
were as limp as noodles.
Finally, I reached land.
I fell asleep right there.

When I woke up,
I could not move
my arms or legs.
I was tied to the ground
by many, many pieces of string.
Who could have done
such a thing?

I felt something
moving up my leg.
It moved up to my belly.
Could it be a bird?
A rat?

No!

It was a tiny man

no bigger than my hand.

I thought I must be dreaming.

When I woke up again,
I was on a platform with wheels.
It was being pulled by
fifteen hundred tiny horses.

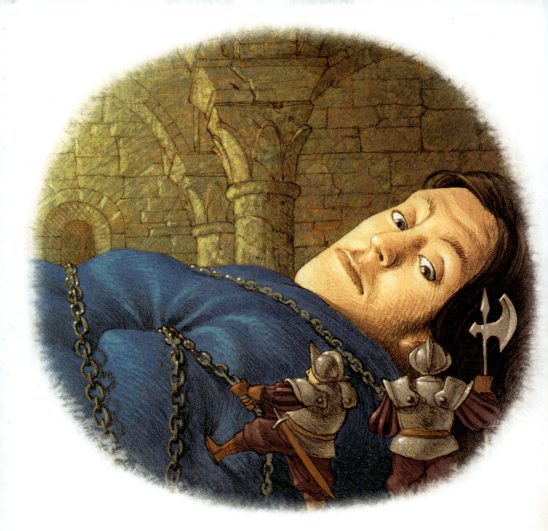

The little people brought me
to an old temple.
They chained me to the wall
with ninety-one tiny chains.
I could not get free!

Many people came
to look at me.
They called me
"the man mountain."
Some of the people were nice.
Other people were mean
and shot me with arrows.

I picked up the mean men.

I put them in my pocket.

I took one out.

I opened my mouth wide.

The people screamed.

I did not eat the wee man.

I put him back on the ground.

The people cheered.

Then the little people
liked me.
They gave me new clothes.
I was too big for them.
So three hundred tailors
sewed me a new suit.

17

The little people gave me food.

I was still hungry.

So they gave me forty sheep

and six cows to eat every day!

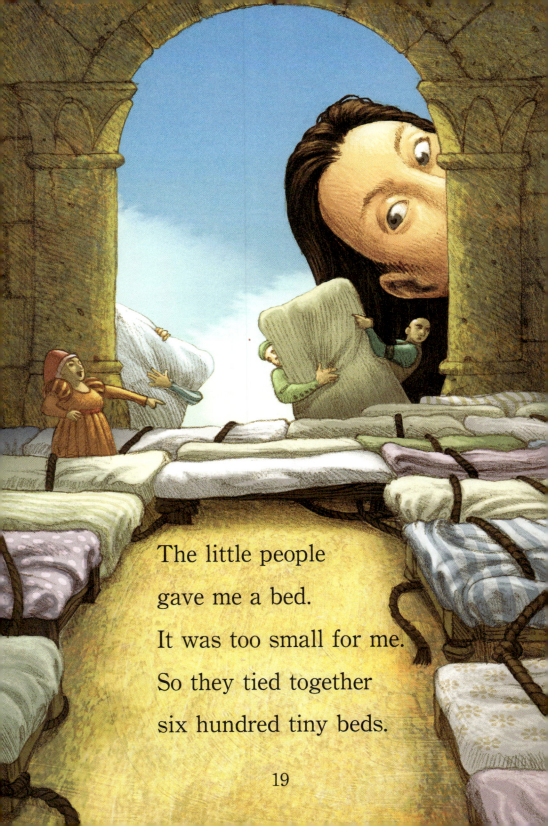

The little people
gave me a bed.
It was too small for me.
So they tied together
six hundred tiny beds.

19

The little people were
not afraid of me anymore.
They danced in my hand.
They played hide-and-seek
in my hair.

Then the little people
had a parade through my legs.

They even taught me
their language.
They told me that their land
was called Lilliput.

But they still would not

set me free.

I had to agree to help them.

I had to help whenever they asked.

I also had to give them

the things in my pockets.

I gave them my comb.

It was too big for their heads.

I gave them my watch.

They were too small to hold it.

They finally took off
my chains!

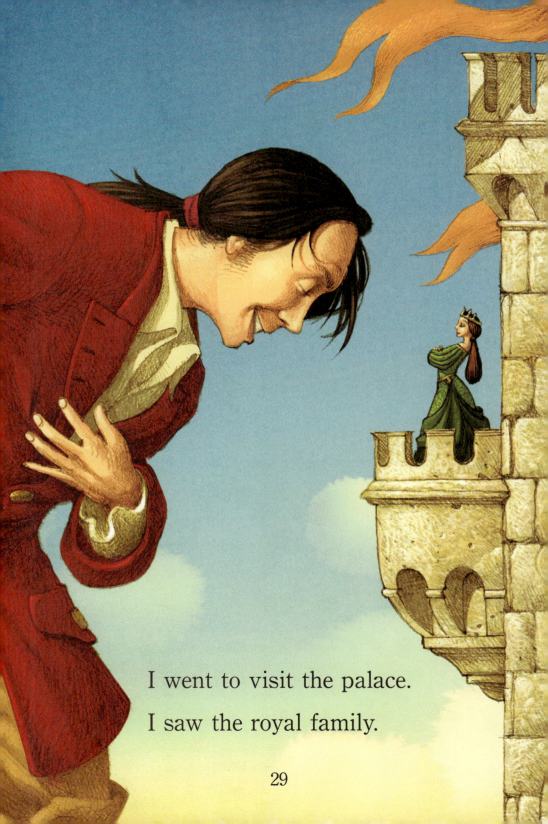

I went to visit the palace.

I saw the royal family.

The people at the palace
danced and jumped on ropes.
The person who jumped the highest
got a great job.

The people there argued
about silly things.
Some said shoes
with low heels were best.
Some said shoes
with high heels were best.

They argued about
which way to crack eggs.
Should eggs be cracked
at the small end?
Or the big end?

The people in Lilliput were Small-Enders. The Big-Enders lived on the next island over. The emperor ordered me to attack the Big-Enders.

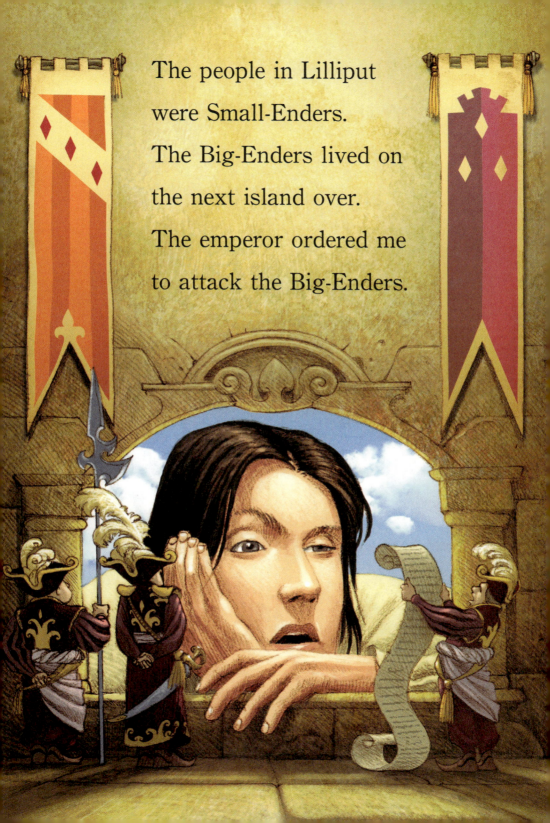

I had a plan.

I wove many tiny ropes

into big ropes.

I attached iron hooks

to the ropes.

I took off
my shoes and stockings.
Then I waded out to sea.

The Big-Enders saw me coming.

They shot arrows at me.

The arrows were too small

to hurt me much.

The Big-Enders were scared.

They jumped off their ships.

I put the hooks on the ships

and dragged them away.

38

I took the ships
back to Lilliput.
The war was over.

I always tried to help
my friends.
One night,
hundreds of little people
woke me up.

There was a fire
at the royal palace.
The empress needed my help!

There was no water
to put out the fire.
So I peed
all over the palace.
The empress was very angry.

The little people

were mad at me

for peeing on the palace.

They did not feed me anymore.

It was time for me

to leave Lilliput.

I found a boat floating
in the ocean.
What luck!
It was the perfect size
for me.

47

Then I sailed off
to my next adventure.